ON LINE

To the memory of Grandma Rose
— S.M.

Go to scholastic.com for web site information on Scholastic authors and illustrators.

Text copyright © 2001 by Scholastic Inc.
Illustrations copyright © 2001 by Hans Wilhelm, Inc.
All rights reserved. Published by Scholastic Inc.
SCHOLASTIC, CARTWHEEL BOOKS, DINOFOURS, and associated logos
are trademarks and/or registered trademarks of Scholastic Inc.

Library of Congress Cataloging-in-Publication Data
Metzger, Steve.
     Dinofours, it's Pumpkin Day! / by Steve Metzger ; illustrated by Hans Wilhelm.
          p. cm. — (Dinofours)
     "Cartwheel Books."
     Summary: Just before Halloween, Albert brings the perfect pumpkin to school and is dismayed when the other students want to turn it into a jack-o'-lantern.
     ISBN 0-439-29569-6 (pbk.)
          [1. Pumpkin — Fiction. 2. Jack-o'-lanterns — Fiction. 3. Halloween — Fiction. 4. Nursery schools — Fiction.
5. Schools — Fiction. 6. Dinosaurs — Fiction.] I. Title: It's Pumpkin Day! II. Wilhelm, Hans, 1945- ill. III. Title.

PZ7.M56775 Dhn 2001
[E] — dc21   2001020033

10 9 8 7 6 5 4 3   01 02 03 04 05
                                                                                                              24
                              Printed in the U.S.A.
                           First printing, October 2001

DINOFOURS®

IT'S PUMPKIN DAY!

by Steve Metzger
Illustrated by Hans Wilhelm

Cartwheel®
·B·O·O·K·S·®

SCHOLASTIC INC.
New York   Toronto   London   Auckland   Sydney
Mexico City   New Delhi   Hong Kong

It was almost Halloween!

On the way to school, Albert and his mother walked past a grocery store.

"Mommy," Albert said, "look at all the pumpkins!" He walked over to the table where the pumpkins were displayed.

"Can I have one?" Albert asked his mother. "Please?"

"Sure," Albert's mother replied. "But right now we're on our way to school."

"That's okay," Albert said. "If we get it now I can show it to my friends."

"All right," said Albert's mother. "Which one would you like?" Albert looked at all the different pumpkins. "I want this one," he said.

Then Albert sang this song:

> *I like this pumpkin best*
> *Of all the ones I see.*
> *It's smooth and round and shiny—*
> *It's just right for me!*

Albert's mother paid for the pumpkin and off they went.

When they arrived at school, Mrs. Dee greeted them.

"My, my, Albert," said Mrs. Dee. "What have you got there?"

"It's my pumpkin!" Albert said. "And it's the best one in the whole world."

"I can see that," said Mrs. Dee. "Would you like to put it on our nature table? I'm sure the other children will really like it, too."

"Yes," Albert said proudly.

Albert's mother said good-bye as Mrs. Dee placed the pumpkin in the middle of the nature table.

Albert spent a few minutes looking at his pumpkin. Then he walked over to the sand table.

Just then, Tara arrived and went straight to the nature table.
"What a nice pumpkin!" she said as she touched it. "It's so smooth."

In a moment, Albert was beside her.

"That's *my* pumpkin!" he said. "You can't touch it."

Mrs. Dee joined them.

"Remember, Albert," said Mrs. Dee. "The nature table is a place for *all* children to explore."

"Oh, all right," Albert said. Turning to Tara he said, "But it's *my* pumpkin—not yours!"

"It's just a *pumpkin*," Tara said as she walked away. Albert turned around and went back to the sand table.

Suddenly Brendan burst through the
classroom door and raced over to the nature table.

"What a cool pumpkin!" he said, lifting it over his
head. "Look at me — I'm strong!"

Once again, Albert immediately appeared.

"Put my pumpkin down!" he said. "You're going to
drop it!"

Mrs. Dee arrived and took the pumpkin away from Brendan.

"Yes," she said. "You need to be careful with objects on the nature table."

Then Mrs. Dee looked at the clock. "Please come to the rug, everybody," she announced. "It's Circle Time. Albert, would you like to bring your pumpkin to Circle Time? It would be great for sharing."

"Uh...okay," Albert said.

After the children sat down, Mrs. Dee said, "We have a special surprise today. Albert, would you like to tell us what you've brought to school?"

Albert's face brightened.

"This is my pumpkin!" he said. "It's smooth and round and—"

"Let's make Albert's pumpkin into a scary jack-o'-lantern for Halloween!" said Brendan.

"That's a great idea," said Tracy. "My big sister has a jack-o'-lantern in her classroom."

Brendan began to chant, "We want a jack-o'-lantern! We want a jack-o'-lantern!"

The other children joined in...except Albert.

"Wait a minute," said Mrs. Dee. "I'm not so sure Albert wants his pumpkin to be made into a jack-o'-lantern. Do you, Albert?"

Everyone looked at Albert, waiting for his answer. "I...I...
I guess so," he said.

"Are you sure?" Mrs. Dee asked.

"Yes," said Albert as he looked at the excited faces of his
classmates.

"Okay," said Mrs. Dee. "Halloween's almost here. And on
that day, we'll make Albert's pumpkin into a jack-o'-lantern."

Albert talked quietly with his pumpkin. "I'm still not sure
I want you to be a jack-o'-lantern," he said. When Circle Time
was over, Albert left to paint at the easel.

Albert had a busy week. He built with blocks, collected acorns outside, and played with clay. But he always found time to visit his pumpkin.

Finally, it was Halloween. Albert still wasn't sure if he wanted his pumpkin to become a jack-o'-lantern.

After a "spooky" story time, Mrs. Dee gathered the children at one of the classroom tables. She placed Albert's pumpkin on a countertop that was safely out of reach of the children.

"Now it's time to make our jack-o'-lantern," said Mrs. Dee as she cut off the top. "I'll make one eye here."

"No!" said Albert, in a loud voice.

Everyone looked at Albert.

"I know how I want my pumpkin to look," he continued. "Please make one eye on the other side. And it should be a triangle eye."

"Okay," said Mrs. Dee, turning the pumpkin around. "Now where should the other eye be?"

"Over there!" Albert said as he pointed to a spot near the first eye.

After Mrs. Dee made the second eye, Albert happily pointed out where and how the nose and mouth should be cut.

After the last piece of the mouth was finished, Mrs. Dee said, "Albert, you've been such a big help. Your pumpkin looks wonderful."

"It's not done yet," Albert said.

"All right," said Mrs. Dee with a smile. "What should I do now?"

"Please make two little rectangles here and there," Albert said, pointing to the bottom corners of the nose.

When Mrs. Dee finished, Albert announced, "That's an A for Albert. Now my jack-o'-lantern's done!"
Everybody cheered...especially Albert.

Then Albert sang this new song:

Mrs. Dee listens
To what I have to say.
I love my pumpkin's brand-new face —
It's even got an A!